PowerKids Readers:

The Bilingual Library of the United States of America™

Bilingual Edition
English/Spanish
Edición bilingüe

OHIO

JENNIFER WAY

TRADUCCIÓN AL ESPAÑOL: MARÍA CRISTINA BRUSCA

The Rosen Publishing Group's
PowerKids Press™ & **Editorial Buenas Letras**™
New York

Published in 2006 by The Rosen Publishing Group, Inc.
29 East 21st Street, New York, NY 10010

First Edition

Library of Congress Cataloging-in-Publication Data

Way, Jennifer.
Ohio / Jennifer Way ; traducción al español, María Cristina Brusca. — 1st ed.
p. cm. — (The bilingual library of the United States of America) Includes bibliographical references and index.
ISBN 1-4042-3100-5 (library binding)
1. Ohio—Juvenile literature. I. Title. II. Series.
F491.3.W39 2006
977.1—dc22
                                                    2005020506

Manufactured in the United States of America

Due to the changing nature of Internet links, Editorial Buenas Letras has developed an online list of Web sites related to the subject of this book. This site is updated regularly. Please use this link to access the list:

http://www.buenasletraslinks.com/ls/ohio

Contents

Contenido

Welcome to Ohio

Ohio is the thirty-fourth largest state in the United States. Ohio is known as the Buckeye State. The buckeye is Ohio's state tree.

Bienvenidos a Ohio

Por su tamaño, Ohio ocupa el lugar treinta y cuatro entre los estados de los Estados Unidos. Ohio es conocido como el Estado *Buckeye*. El *buckeye*, o castaño de Indias, es el árbol oficial de Ohio.

Ohio Flag and State Seal

Bandera y escudo de Ohio

Ohio Geography

Ohio is in the Midwest of the United States. Ohio borders the states of Indiana, Kentucky, Michigan, Pennsylvania, and West Virginia.

Geografía de Ohio

Ohio está en la región central de los Estados Unidos, conocida como el *Midwest*. Ohio linda con los estados de Indiana, Kentucky, Michigan, Pensilvania y Virginia Occidental.

Lake Erie
Lago Erie

MICHIGAN

PENNSYLVANIA
PENSILVANIA

Cleveland

Youngstown
Akron

Toledo

Canton

Mansfield

OHIO

Columbus

WEST VIRGINIA
VIRGINIA OCCIDENTAL

INDIANA

Dayton

Ohio River
Río Ohio

Cincinnati

KENTUCKY

Map Key
Claves del mapa

Major City
Ciudad principal

Capital
Capital

River
Río

Map of Ohio

Mapa de Ohio

Ohio has rolling hills and flat plains. Lake Erie is in the north of the state. Lake Erie is one of the five Great Lakes.

En Ohio hay colinas y grandes llanuras. En el norte del estado se encuentra el lago Erie. El lago Erie es uno de los cinco Grandes Lagos.

Lake Erie in Northern Ohio

Lago Erie, en el extremo norte de Ohio

Ohio History

The first people to live in Ohio were Native Americans. They came to Ohio more than 2,000 years ago. Some of these people, such as the Adena and the Hopewell, built mounds.

Historia de Ohio

Los primeros pobladores de Ohio fueron los nativos americanos. Llegaron a Ohio hace más de 2,000 años. Algunos de estos grupos, como los Adena y los Hopewell, construyeron montículos.

Serpent Mound in Spring, Ohio

Montículo de la Serpiente, en Spring, Ohio

Ulysses S. Grant was a general during the Civil War. The Civil War was fought from 1861 to 1865. Grant became the first U.S. president born in Ohio. He was president from 1869 until 1877.

Ulysses S. Grant fue general durante la Guerra. La Guerra Civil tuvo lugar entre 1861 y 1865. Grant se convirtió en el primer presidente de E.U.A. nacido en Ohio. Grant fue presidente de 1869 a 1877.

General Ulysses S. Grant

General Ulysses S. Grant

Orville and Wilbur Wright grew up in Dayton, Ohio. On December 17, 1903, they became the first people to fly an airplane. The flight lasted 12 seconds and covered 120 feet (36.5 m).

Orville y Wilbur Wright crecieron en Dayton, Ohio. El 17 de diciembre de 1903 se convirtieron en las primeras personas en volar con éxito en un aeroplano. El vuelo duró 12 segundos y atravesó una distancia de 120 pies (36.5 m).

The Wright Brothers and Their Airplane Named the *Flyer*

Los hermanos Wright y su avión, llamado *Flyer* (Volador)

Maya Lin was born in Athens, Ohio, in 1959. She is an artist and architect. Her most famous work is the Vietnam Veterans Memorial in Washington, D.C. Lin planned it when she was only 22 years old!

Maya Lin nació en Athens, Ohio, en 1959. Lin es artista y arquitecta. Su obra más famosa es el Monumento a los Veteranos de Vietnam, que está en Washington, D.C. ¡Lin diseñó este monumento cuando tenía sólo 22 años!

Maya Lin

Vietnam Veterans Memorial

Monumento a los Veteranos de Vietnam

Living in Ohio

People from all over the world have settled in Ohio. There are events throughout the state where people honor the countries their families came from.

La vida en Ohio

En Ohio vive gente de todo el mundo. Por todo el estado hay eventos donde la gente celebra a los países de los que provienen sus familias.

Pumpkin Festival in Hanna, Ohio

Festival de la calabaza en Hanna, Ohio

Ohio has the largest number of Amish people in the United States. The Amish are a religious group. They do not use most machines, such as cars. They travel by horse and buggy.

En Ohio vive el mayor número de Amish de los Estados Unidos.
Los Amish son un grupo religioso.
Los Amish no usan muchas máquinas, como los automóviles. Los Amish viajan en carretas, tiradas por caballos.

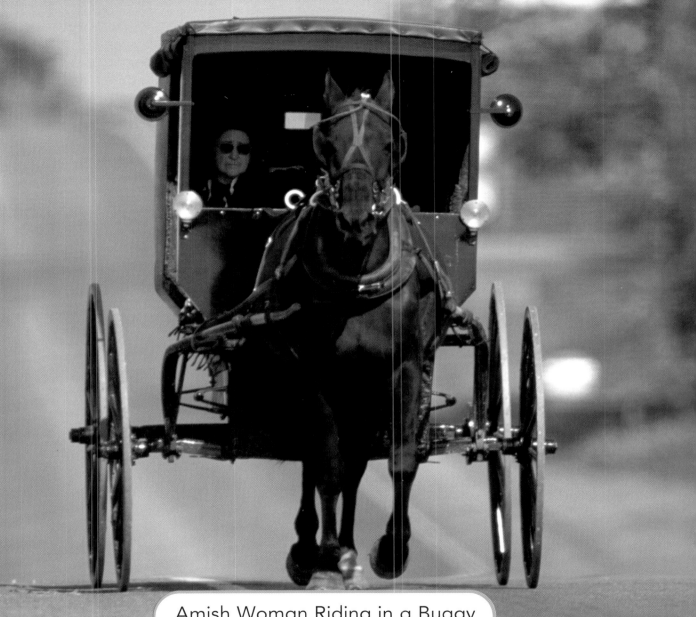

Amish Woman Riding in a Buggy

Una mujer Amish en su carruaje

Ohio Today

The Rock and Roll Hall of Fame and Museum is in Cleveland, Ohio. It opened in 1995. People come to the museum from all over the world to learn about the history of rock music.

Ohio, hoy

En Cleveland, Ohio, está el Museo y Galería de la Fama del Rock and Roll. Se inauguró en 1995. Gente de todo el mundo visita el museo para aprender sobre la historia de la música rock.

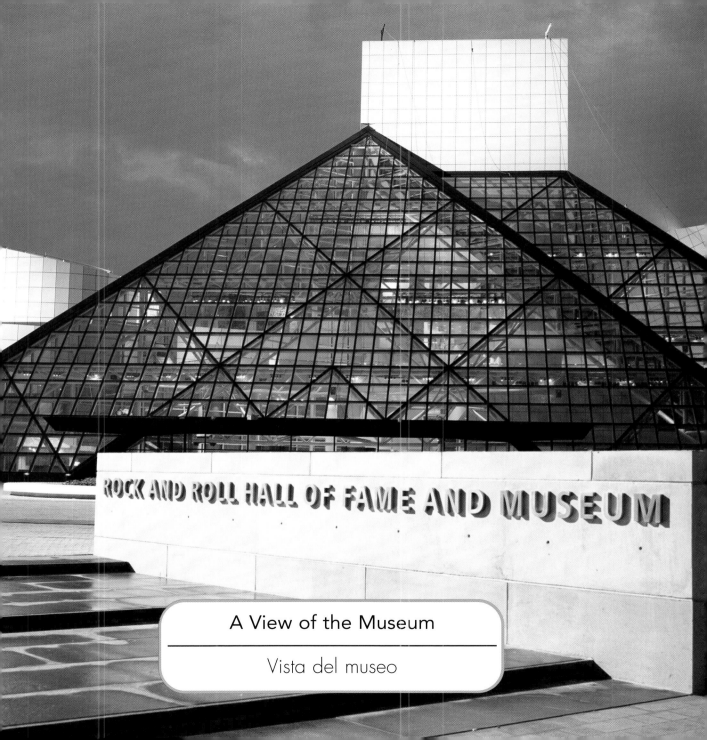

ROCK AND ROLL HALL OF FAME AND MUSEUM

A View of the Museum

Vista del museo

Columbus, Cincinnati, Cleveland, and Toledo are the biggest cities in Ohio. Columbus is the capital of the state of Ohio.

Columbus, Cincinnati, Cleveland y Toledo son las ciudades más grandes de Ohio. Columbus es la capital del estado de Ohio.

The Ohio Statehouse in Columbus

Casa de gobierno en Columbus

Activity:
Let's Draw the Ohio Flag

Actividad:
Dibujemos la bandera de Ohio

1

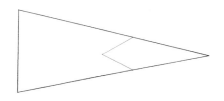

To draw Ohio's flag, begin by drawing a triangle on its side. Draw a *V* on its side, inside the triangle.

Para dibujar la bandera de Ohio comienza por trazar un triángulo. Luego dibuja una *V* apuntando a la izquierda dentro del triángulo.

2

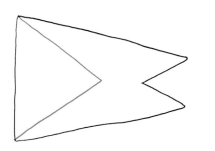

Erase extra lines. Now you have the bird's-tail shape of the flag. Draw a triangle inside the flag.

Borra las líneas sobrantes. Ahora, ya tienes una bandera en forma de cola de ave. Dibuja un triángulo dentro de la bandera.

3

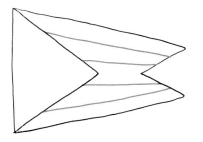

Add four lines. You will color in the space between them later to make the flag's red and white stripes.

Agrega cuatro líneas. Cuando colorees la bandera, éstas serán las barras rojas y blancas.

4

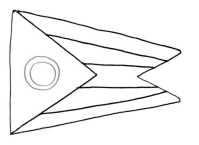

Add an O to the center of the inner triangle.

Dibuja una O en el centro del triángulo interior.

5

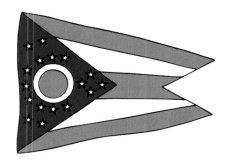

Draw 17 small stars around the O. Color in your flag.

Alrededor de la O dibuja 17 estrellas pequeñas. Colorea tu bandera.

Timeline

Cronología

Adena and Hopewell Native Americans build mounds in central and southwest Ohio.	**800 B.C.– 500 A.D. 800 a.C.– 500 d.C.**	Los grupos nativoamericanos Adena y Hopewell construyen montículos en el centro y el sudoeste de Ohio.
René-Robert Cavelier explores the area and claims it for France.	**1670**	René-Robert Cavelier explora y reclama la región para Francia.
Britain claims Ohio.	**1750**	Gran Bretaña reclama Ohio.
Ohio becomes part of the Northwest Territory of the United States.	**1787**	Ohio pasa a ser parte del Territorio Noroccidental de los Estados Unidos.
Ohio becomes the seventeenth state.	**1803**	Ohio se convierte en el estado diecisiete.
Columbus is named capital of Ohio.	**1816**	Se nombra a Columbus capital del estado.
Oberlin College is founded. It is the first college in the country to admit women and African Americans.	**1833**	Se funda Oberlin College. Ésta es la primera universidad del país en admitir mujeres y afroamericanos.
The Cincinnati Redstockings become the first professional baseball team. They are later renamed the Cincinnati Reds.	**1869**	Los Cincinnati Redstockings se convierten en el primer equipo profesional de béisbol. Luego serán renombrados los Cincinnati Reds.
Neil Armstrong, of Wapakoneta, Ohio, becomes the first man to walk on the Moon.	**1969**	Neil Armstrong, nativo de Wapakoneta, Ohio, es el primer hombre en caminar en la Luna.

28

Ohio Events

Eventos en Ohio

March Hinckley Buzzard Day in Hinckley	Marzo Día de los buitres, en Hinckley
May Utica Old Fashioned Ice Cream Festival in Utica Moon When the Ponies Shed Festival in Hilliard Asian Festival in Columbus	Mayo Festival del helado tradicional de Utica, en Utica Festival de la luna del cambio de pelaje de los ponis, en Hilliard Festival asiático, en Columbus
June Irish summer Festival in Euclid Festival Latino in Columbus Parade the Circle Celebration in Cleveland	Junio Festival irlandés de verano, en Euclid Festival latino, en Columbus Desfile artístico en el Museo de las Artes de Cleveland
July Jazz and Rib Fest in Columbus	Julio Festival de jazz y barbacoa, en Columbus
August Sweet Corn Festival in Millersport Carnation Festival in Alliance	Agosto Festival del elote, en Millersport Festival del clavel escarlata, en Alliance
September German Village Oktoberfest in Columbus Ohio Swiss Festival in Sugarcreek	Septiembre Oktoberfest de la aldea alemana, en Columbus Festival suizo de Ohio, en Sugarcreek
October Cincinnati Flower and Farm Fest in Cincinnati Middfest International Festival in Middletown	Octubre Festival de las flores y granjas, en Cincinnati Festival internacional Middfest, en Middletown

Ohio Facts/Datos sobre Ohio

Population
11.4 million

Población
11.4 millones

Capital
Columbus

Capital
Columbus

State Motto
"With God, all things are possible"

Lema del estado
"Con Dios, todo es posible"

State Flower
Scarlet Carnation

Flor del estado
Clavel escarlata

State Bird
Cardinal

Ave del estado
Cardenal

State Nickname
The Buckeye State

Mote del estado
Estado del Castaño

State Tree
Ohio Buckeye

Árbol del estado
Castaño de Ohio

State Song
"Beautiful Ohio"

Canción del estado
"Hermoso Ohio"

Famous Ohioans/Ohioanos famosos

Thomas Edison
(1847–1931)

Inventor
Inventor

William Howard Taft
(1857–1930)

U.S. President
Presidente de E.U.A.

Warren G. Harding
(1865–1923)

U.S. President
Presidente de E.U.A.

Neil Armstrong
(1930–   )

Astronaut
Astronauta

Toni Morrison
(1931–   )

Author
Escritora

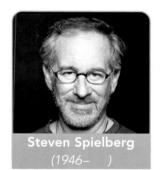

Steven Spielberg
(1946–   )

Director
Director de cine

Words to Know/Palabras que debes saber

<u>border</u>
frontera

<u>buggy</u>
carreta

<u>mounds</u>
montículos

<u>museum</u>
museo

Here are more books to read about Ohio:
Otros libros que puedes leer sobre Ohio:

In English/En inglés:

Ohio
By Brown, Dottie
Lerner Publications, 2001

Ohio
By Sherrow, Victoria
Benchmark Books, 1998

Words in English: 320

Palabras en español: 352

Index

Índice